Are You My Lover?

A Journey To Finding The One

by Dr. Kezia Shine

Are You My Lover?

by Dr. Kezia Shine

TruthWorks
Publishing™

Introduction

We are Be-ings inhabiting the human experience, navigating through the complexities of relationships, love, and self-discovery. This journey is not about mere connection with others, but about deepening the connection with ourselves. Every person we encounter is a mirror reflecting something back to us — our fears, our wounds, our hidden strengths, and the parts of ourselves we have yet to embrace.

It is natural to seek a partner who aligns with our desires, needs, and values. Yet, many times, we find ourselves drawn to individuals who challenge us, frustrate us, or even break us open in ways we never expected. These relationships, even the painful ones, serve a higher purpose. They are not mistakes, nor are they failures. They are teachers.

In this book, we explore the various personalities we meet along the way — the Adventurer, the Poet, the Protector, the Party Lover, the Storm, and the Narcissist. While these labels help illustrate their characteristics, they are not meant to define them as "good" or "bad."

No person is solely one thing. We are all evolving, shifting, and growing. Every individual is on their own path, learning their own lessons, and awakening in their own time. It is not our place to judge where they are, just as we would not want to be judged for where we are on our journey.

Instead of seeing relationships as "right" or "wrong," what if we saw them as tools for inner work? What if we approached every experience with the understanding that it is here to teach us something? Perhaps we were meant to learn boundaries, or self-worth, or unconditional love. Perhaps we needed to see our patterns, our fears, and our conditioned beliefs that keep us repeating cycles. Every partner we encounter, whether they stay or leave, has played a role in shaping who we are becoming.

The deeper we go into this journey, the more we realize that love is not something we should seek outside of ourselves. It is not about finding "the one" who completes us. It is about stripping away the illusions, the attachments, and the expectations so that we can return to our own wholeness. True love begins within. When we release the need for another to fill the spaces within us, we begin to operate from a place of authenticity rather than lack.

This book is not a guide to finding the perfect partner. It is an invitation to embark on a journey within — to uncover the lessons hidden in each relationship, to heal the parts of yourself that long for attention, and to step into the fullness of your Be-ing. As you read, I invite you to reflect on your own experiences, to release resentment, to embrace gratitude, and to find the gift in every soul who has walked alongside you, even if only for a moment.

Through each personality, may you become freer of the human constraints that bind you. May you step into the present moment with clarity, love, and unwavering truth. May you remember that your soul's purpose is not to find love — it is to Be Love. And when you arrive at that place within yourself, the world reflects it back to you in ways more beautiful than you could have ever imagined.

Welcome to the journey home — to yourself!

ONCE UPON A TIME,
IN A WORLD SO WIDE,
LIVED A GIRL WITH A OPEN HEART.
EAGER TO LIVE
AND A ZEST FOR LIFE,
SHE DREAMED OF FINDING
HER PERFECT PARTNER.

SHE LISTENED FOR YEARS,
AND HEARD ALL THE FEARS
OF HER LOVED ONES AND THE WORLD AROUND.
THEY SAID FINDING THE ONE
IS WHAT NEEDS TO BE DONE
BECAUSE THAT IS WHAT LIFE'S ALL ABOUT.

SO SHE DREAMED OF LOVE,
OF FINDING "THE ONE",
AND SET OUT ON HER QUEST.
HER MIND TELLING HER
IT HAD TO BE DONE,
THAT THIS ROUTE WAS THE BEST!

"Are you My Lover?"
she would ask on her way.
She would question as she searched
all of the day.

In coffee shops, restaurants,
concerts, and gyms,
Hangouts with friends,
Where could she find him?

She even searched
on the internet
Hoping to find him
Wherever she went.

ADVENTURE

She first met the Adventurer.
He was wild and free.
He climbed up mountains,
And swam deep in the sea.

He ran so fast
She could barely keep pace,
Constantly feeling
The never ending race.

Every second she pushed
To be better and better.
Thinking love shouldn't feel
Like this constant pressure.

"ARE YOU MY LOVER?"
SHE ASKED WITH A SIGH.
HE GRINNED AND SAID,
"ONLY IF YOU CAN FLY!"

BUT SHE WASN'T MEANT
TO CHASE OR TO FLEE,
SO SHE WAVED GOODBYE
AND THEN LET HIM BE.

THEN SHE MET THE POET,
SO SOFT AND SO DEEP.
HIS WORDS WERE LIKE MAGIC,
THEY MADE HER HEART LEAP.

HE WROTE OF THE STARS,
OF PASSION AND ART.
BUT SHE FELT UNSEEN,
BY THE DEPTHS OF HIS HEART.

HIS POETIC PASSION
OUTWEIGHED HIS DRIVE FOR A PARTNER.
HE WAS ONLY IN LOVE
WITH HIS SKILL AS A CHARMER.

"Are you My Lover?"
she whispered one night.
He sighed and said,
"only by the moonlight."

But she needed love
that stayed in the day.
So with a hug and a smile,
she walked away.

THEN THERE WAS THE PROTECTOR,
HE WAS BOLD AND STRONG.
A SHIELD OF SAFETY,
WHERE NOTHING FELT WRONG.

HE BUILT A WALL SO HIGH,
KEPT HER LOCKED IN TIGHT,
SHE LONGED FOR FREEDOM
TO RETURN TO HER FLIGHT.

SHE HAD SLOWLY LOST FRIENDS,
AND MADE HIM HER LIFE.
SHE HAD ALLOWED HIM TO CAPTURE
AND STEAL ALL HER LIGHT.

"Are You My Lover?"
She asked in despair.
He said, "Only if
You stay right here."

Love should always
Let you spread your wings,
Not keep you bound
By golden strings.

She found a way
To unlock all her chains
Running as fast as she could.
Leaving behind
The aches and the pains
Of being so misunderstood.

She then met Party Lover,
Wild and loud.
Always surrounded
by a fun-loving crowd.

She felt how nice it was
to be wild and free,
After escaping
not allowed "to be Me".

Glasses raised high,
Dancing past the dawn.
But when the sun rose,
She found his light gone.

"Are you My Lover?"
she asked through the night.
He laughed and said,
"only when it feels right!"

Love should not be
A fleeting escape
so she left him there.
to be bent out of shape.

Next she met the Storm,
He was both high and low,
One day all sunshine,
Next day full of woe.

His love was a thrill,
A passionate ride.
But she never knew
Who she'd find inside.

He gave her a ring
Which made her dream,
Her open heart really cared
But then he crashed
And her dream was dashed
Her soul told her she should not dare.

"Are you my lover?"
she asked with a tear.
He smiled, then raged,
then he disappeared.

Love should not be
a guessing game,
so she walked away
and kept her own name.

One day, she met
the Narcissist's charm.
He took her hand,
kept her safe from harm.

His words were sweet,
his eyes pulled her in.
Love to him was a game,
she could never win.

She pushed and she pulled,
tried to crack him open.
But his will was solid
and his heart was frozen.

He thought he was perfect,
no interest in feeling.
So she left on a journey
for her heart to find healing.

"Are you My Lover?"
she asked with doubt.
He laughed and whispered,
"You can't live without."

Love should never
make you feel small.
So she broke from her cage
and stood straight and tall.

She cried and she healed,
She danced and she grew.
She found herself
And her heart felt brand new.

Just when she thought
That her search was done,
A blind date appeared,
Just one last one.

SHE OPENED THE DOOR,
HER HEART OPEN WIDE,
BUT THERE WAS NO ONE
STANDING OUTSIDE.

INSTEAD, A MIRROR,
SHINING SO BRIGHT,
REFLECTING HER STRENGTH,
HER LOVE AND HER LIGHT.

"ARE YOU MY LOVER?"
SHE ASKED WITH A GRIN.
THE GIRL IN THE MIRROR
JUST SAID, "LOOK WITHIN!"

SHE SMILED SO BIG,
FOR SHE FINALLY KNEW
YOUR PERFECT LOVER
IS INSIDE OF YOU!!!!

The Journey to Finding Yourself

Once upon a time, we were told that love was something to be found. That somewhere, out there, in the vastness of the world, there was a perfect person who would make us whole. A soulmate. A missing piece.

So, like many before her, our heroine set out on a quest. She searched for love in the thrill of adventure, in the depths of poetry, in the arms of protectors, in the glow of parties, and in the chaos of storms. She chased love through highs and lows, through passion and pain, through whispers and lies.

But every love left her longing. Every "almost" turned into "not quite." Every hand she held felt like trying to grasp the wind. She searched and searched, until exhaustion weighed heavy on her soul.

Then, one day, when she had nothing left to give, she looked into the mirror.

And there, in her own reflection, she found the love she had been searching for all along.

This is a story about the journey we all take — not to find someone else, but to find ourselves.

Because the greatest love story you will ever live is the one where you finally fall in love with you.

And that, dear reader, is where the magic begins.

WITH LOVE,
DR SHINE

About The Author

Dr. Kezia Shine shows up playing various roles in this experience:

- loving Mom
- caring Chiropractor
- empathetic Energy Healer
- thoughtful Mentor
- motivated Public Speaker
- inspiring Life Coach

It is her mission to help guide those who are stuck in a limiting belief pattern to move into a love-based consciousness way of living.

For more information, check out her website:
https://www.drshinekc.com/

TruthWorks
Publishing™

www.ingramcontent.com/pod-product-compliance
Lightning Source LLC
Chambersburg PA
CBRC090958100726
47911CB00011B/188